Our Corner
Grocery Store

Our Corner Grocery Store

Joanne Schwartz Illustrated by Laura Beingessner

TUNDRA BOOKS

Published in Canada by Tundra Books,
75 Sherbourne Street, Toronto, Ontario M5A 2P9

Published in the United States by Tundra Books of Northern New York,
P.O. Box 1030, Plattsburgh, New York 12901

Library of Congress Control Number: 2008903011

Library and Archives Canada Cataloguing in Publication
Schwartz, Joanne F., 1960-
Our corner grocery store / Joanne Schwartz ; Laura Beingessner,
illustrator.
ISBN 978-0-88776-868-2 (bound)
I. Beingessner, Laura, 1965- II. Title.
PS8637.C592O97 2009   jC813'.6   C2008-902102-9

ONTARIO ARTS COUNCIL
CONSEIL DES ARTS DE L'ONTARIO

We acknowledge the financial support of the Government of Canada through the Book Publishing Industry Development Program (BPIDP)
and that of the Government of Ontario through the Ontario Media Development Corporation's Ontario Book Initiative.
We further acknowledge the support of the Canada Council for the Arts and the Ontario Arts Council for our publishing program.

Printed and bound in China

1   2   3   4   5   6   14   13   12   11   10   09

For Rachel and Sophie,

my most precious community,

and to the real Domenico and Rosa,

who made their community

a wonderful place to grow up in.

— J.S.

For my son, Emilio.

— L.B.

Saturday is my favorite day of the week. I spend every Saturday at my Nonno Domenico and Nonna Rosa's corner grocery store.

It's early in the morning when I arrive. Mrs. Mele is out walking her dog. Once in a while a car goes by, but mostly it's quiet. The neighborhood is still asleep.

Nonno Domenico is busy getting ready for his customers. "*Buon giorno*," he says. "Are you all set to work, Anna Maria?"

Nonna Rosa hugs and kisses me and hurries me into the kitchen behind the store. "You must eat a good breakfast if you are to help your nonno and me all day." We all have jobs at our corner grocery store.

At eight o'clock we open the store. Nonna Rosa turns on the lights and unlocks the door. Nonno Domenico arranges the fruit and vegetables on the wooden racks. I run outside to help him. On one side we have the apples, oranges, pears, bananas, and strawberries. On the other side are tomatoes and cucumbers, broccoli and green beans. I make sure everything is in neat rows, while Nonno Domenico writes the prices on little cardboard signs.

There are only two short aisles in our corner grocery store. When I come inside, I have to close the door before I can get to the counter. If I walk down one aisle and come back up the other, I have made a little square, and I'm right back where I started. The store is tiny, but the shelves are packed with many surprises.

Sometimes when I visit, Nonno has brand-new paint sets with six round pots of color and tiny paintbrushes. Today I see birthday candles and party hats. Umbrellas and shoelaces hang from the ceiling. Flat, round pizza pans are stacked up high on the shelf, and bright, yellow sponges dangle in the window.

The sun has climbed higher in the sky. The bread delivery has come, and it's my job to sort it on the shelf. There are crusty buns for sandwiches and long sticks called baguettes that look like swords. There are round loaves like doughnuts with holes in the middle and chewy cornbread that looks like big, flat stones. That's Nonna Rosa's favorite, and I take one to the kitchen so she can have a slice with her morning coffee.

My friend Charlie comes by with two big pieces of fat chalk.
We draw pictures all along the sidewalk, from the store to
Charlie's house and back.

At noon the store is filled with hungry kids. Everyone in the neighborhood loves my Nonno Domenico's sandwiches. He asks them what kind they would like.

"*Provolone*, please," someone calls. "*Mortadella* and *Havarti* for me," somebody else says.

Nonno Domenico switches on the slicing machine and thin, round circles of meat or cheese fall onto the scale. He piles them on a crusty bun and wraps the sandwich to go. When the busy lunch hour is over, Nonno makes a sandwich just for me. I bite into it and crumbs scatter over my shirt. The creamy cheese and salty meat taste fresh and delicious.

By three o'clock, the milk truck arrives. The side door slides open and I see crates of milk stacked high. While Nonno is busy with the delivery, a group of friends comes in for an afternoon treat.

I stand beside Nonna Rosa and watch them talking and laughing. They crowd around the counter, looking at the candy. There are super-sour sticks, strawberry yumi-yums, candy necklaces, licorice, lollipops, and bubblegum. I look at Nonna Rosa. She winks at me, and then I know I can pick something too.

At four thirty, Nonna Rosa starts dinner. Today I stand beside her on a big, wooden chair and stir the vegetables in the pot.

Good smells drift into the store. When customers come in they smile and say, "Oh! What is Rosa cooking tonight?" Nonno says she is making stuffed mushrooms and then he tells them how to do it.

"Scoop out the insides of the mushrooms and sauté them with breadcrumbs, garlic, herbs, and onions. Mix in grated cheese and a beaten egg to make it stick together. Then stuff the mixture back into the mushroom caps and bake them in the oven." Nonno Domenico brings his fingers to his lips and kisses them. "*Mmm. Delizioso!*"

Scoop out the insides...

chop them up...

add the garlic, bread crumbs, and cheese ...

stuff into caps...

bake...

"mmm **delizioso**"

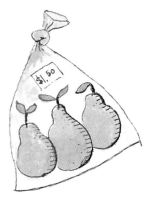  

At five o'clock there are lots of people in the store. Nonno Domenico and Nonna Rosa and I are very busy. There is a lineup, but nobody minds. Everyone says "Hello," "*Ciao*," "Nice to see you, Rosa," "How are you, Anna Maria?"

Nonno weighs the fruit and vegetables, I pass the bags to Nonna, and she works the cash register. Nonno Domenico tells everyone that lettuce is only a dollar now, and the strawberries are two pints for the price of one.

After dinner, kids come in for dessert. In the hot weather, the freezer is full of cold treats. The Freezies stand like tall, colored pencils – red, yellow, blue, and purple. There are ice-cream sandwiches, Drumsticks, and Popsicles. As I poke around, the cold air cools my face. I choose two blue Freezies – one for me and one for Charlie – then I skip down the street to his house. We sit on the steps, slurping the sweet, blue juice and telling each other stories.

When we are finished, I wave good-bye to Charlie and run back to the store to help clean up. All the buns are gone and so is most of the bread. We sold lots of tomatoes and lettuce today, and every single box of strawberries.

There won't be many more customers now. One comes late for a bit of sliced meat, another for some juice and cookies. Mrs. Mele is the last. She buys three bananas and some milk, while I watch her dog. I tell him he's a good boy, and he wags his tail back and forth.

Then they are gone. I sit alone and watch the sun set. The neighborhood is quiet again, and I am sleepy after my busy day. Nonno sees me yawn and calls me in. He turns off the lights and locks the door. Our corner grocery store will open again tomorrow, but for now Nonno Domenico, Nonna Rosa, and I are saying goodnight.

Ciao!